MR. MEN
LITTLE MISS
Fire Station

Roger Hargreaves

Original concept by
Roger Hargreaves

Written and illustrated by
Adam Hargreaves

EGMONT

Mr Lazy had decided to start a business ironing shirts.

He began with great enthusiasm, but after ironing one cuff on one shirt he suddenly felt very tired and decided he needed a nap.

However, he forgot to turn off the iron!

Luckily Little Miss Lucky was walking past his house and when she saw smoke billowing out of Mr Lazy's window she called the emergency services and the operator alerted the fire station.

The alarm bell clanged in the fire station and stirred all the firefighters into instant action.

First down the fire pole was Officer Rush.

But as fast as Officer Rush rushed, Officer Magic was always the first into the engine cab.

"How do you do that?" cried Officer Rush.

There was always a bit of a wait while Officer Muddle sorted himself out.

Now, there are many things in life that should not be rushed, but driving a fire engine is not one of them.

Officer Rush drove out of the station and roared up the road.

He pressed the siren button, but nothing happened.

Luckily, Officer Noisy was on duty.

"OUT OF THE WAY!" he bellowed.

I think he was even louder than the siren!

When they got to the fire, Officer Tickle's extraordinarily long arms caused all sorts of problems with unrolling the hose.

But then they came in
very useful.

Unlike Officer Wrong.

That's the wrong house, Officer Wrong!

Officer Strong climbed the
ladder and rescued Mr Lazy
from an open window.

Officer Rush rushed into the burning building and rescued a pet dog. Officer Magic rescued a cat, a budgerigar, a goldfish and a hamster.

"How do you do that?" cried Officer Rush.

And Officer Nonsense broke down the back door and rescued …

... a pot plant!

Thankfully they had arrived in time to put the fire out.

Thankfully they had not waited for Officer Late!

The firefighters had successfully dealt with another emergency. But as you can imagine, everything needs to be well organised for them to do so.

All the equipment has to be ready and in its place because the fire officers never know when they will be needed.

They have to be set for action at a moment's notice.

And Station Manager Neat was just the right person for this job.

Her Fire Station ran like a well-oiled machine.

Well, most of the time!

It would not be any good if they had not filled the water bowser.

Like Officer Dotty.

Or if they brought the wrong ladder.

Like Officer Wrong.

Or, even worse, if they had forgotten where they had parked the fire engine.

Like Officer Forgetful!

The firefighters didn't only have to be ready for house fires. There were lots of different types of fires they had to put out.

There were forest fires.

And chemical fires which had to be put out using foam.

And sometimes they did not fight fires because there were lots of other emergencies they were called out for.

Like when Mr Greedy got stuck in his car.

I think Mr Greedy needs to buy a bigger car!

Or like when Mr Mean's water pipe froze and burst and the fire officers had to pump out his flooded house.

I think Mr Mean needs to turn his heating on!

They even rescued cats stuck in trees!

"How do you do that?"
cried Officer Rush.

MEOW!

When they got back to the Fire Station after their long, hard day, everyone trudged wearily up the stairs to wash and have supper.

Everyone, that is, except for Officer Magic.

She did not walk up the stairs.

She slid *up* the fire pole!

"How do you do that?" cried Officer Rush.

Suddenly, the alarm rang again and they all had to rush to the scene of another fire.

They arrived at Mr Worry's house who was frantically running around outside shouting, "FIRE! FIRE! FIRE!"

Mr Rush rushed into the house to be confronted by ...

... a slice of burnt toast!

It was a false alarm.